To Marija, Brandon, Evan, and Baby Archer,
and to busy babies everywhere
P. A.

For Nana
H. W.

Text copyright © 2007 by Peggy Archer
Illustrations copyright © 2007 by Hanako Wakiyama

"First Steps" and "Baby Eyes" originally appeared in *Babybug* magazine.
"Twos" originally appeared in *Ladybug* magazine.

First edition 2007

Library of Congress Cataloging-in-Publication Data is available.

Library of Congress Catalog Card Number 2006051832

ISBN 978-0-7636-2467-5

10 9 8 7 6 5 4 3 2 1

Printed in Singapore

This book was typeset in New Century Schoolbook.
The illustrations were done in oil on paper.

Candlewick Press
2067 Massachusetts Avenue
Cambridge, Massachusetts 02140

visit us at www.candlewick.com

FROM DAWN TO DREAMS

Poems for Busy Babies

PEGGY ARCHER

illustrated by HANAKO WAKIYAMA

CANDLEWICK PRESS
CAMBRIDGE, MASSACHUSETTS

Good Morning, Baby!

Wake with the sun.

S t r e t c h   to the sky.

Yawn like the rose

with dew in her eye.

Laugh with the breeze

that dances at dawn.

Sing with the robin

a good-morning song.

Messy Baby

Sippy, drippy apple juice
Dribbling down my chin.
Slurpy, burpy.
Icky sticky.
Big, sloppy grin!

Munchy, crunchy cracker crumbs
Dropping in my lap.
Itchy, scritchy.
Crumby tummy.
Giggle! Clap, clap!

Mushy, slushy cereal—
Oops—I got my nose!
Mishy, mashy.
Squishy, squashy.
Head to my toes!

First Steps

Step, wiggle, wobble.

Step, plop, fall.

Walking is fun,

But I'm faster when I crawl.

Twos

A pair of socks.
A pair of shoes.
Like my feet,
They come in twos.

Slippers, boots,
Or skates that glide.
Left foot, right foot,
Side by side.

Giggles

Wiggle my ears
And wiggle my nose,
'Cause wiggles make giggles—
That's how it goes.

Tickle my tummy,
Tickle my toes,
'Cause tickles make giggles—
Everyone knows.

Wiggle me, tickle me,

Giggle me, oh!

Makes me feel happy,

Head to my toes!

One-Baby Band

One day I found a little door,

Right next to the kitchen floor.

It opened wide—

I looked inside—

Lids and pots and pans I found.

A wooden spoon to make some sound.

Crash! Bang!

Rat-a-tat!

I'm a one-baby band

In a little tin hat!

Sunny Day Friend

I swing,
You swing,
    one, two, three.
Sit, crawl,
Bounce a ball,
    shadow and me!
Hide
In the shade
    of the big oak tree.
Shh!
Silly shadow
    can't find me!

Baby Eyes

Baby eyes,
What can you do?

Open, close
For peekaboo.
Blink and wink,
Then look and see
Someone looking
Back at me!

Kitty on the Sofa

Kitty on the sofa,
Quiet as can be.
Doesn't move a whisker,
Looking at me.

Climbing on the sofa,
Careful as can be . . .
    Up I go!
    Too slow!
Kitty jumps free.

Naptime Friends

Open your eyes, Puppy.

Don't go to sleep.

Open your mouth, Puppy.

Let's see your teeth.

Stick out your tongue, Puppy.

Give me a lick.

Roll on your back, Puppy.

Show me a trick.

You just won't wake up, Puppy!

What can I do?

If you'll be my pillow,

I'll take a nap, too.

Buckled Up

All buckled up
In my own little seat.
The car hums soft and low.
We're headed straight for
The grocery store
As over the road we go.

We'll buy some crackers
And maybe some juice,
And then we'll head back home.
All buckled up
In my own little seat
As over the road we roam.

Piggyback Ride

I like riding piggyback

Up on PapPap's shoulders.

I can see over everyone—

       so tall I almost touch the sun!—

When I ride piggyback.

I like bucking-bronco rides
Up on Daddy's back.
I hold on tight, and off we go—
    racing and bucking, high and low!—
Me and my bucking bronco.

I like getting horsey rides
On my brother's foot.
Giddy-up, horsey, please don't stop—
    galloping faster, *clippety-clop!*—
'Cause I like horsey rides!

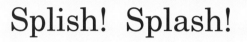

Splish! Splash!

Splish! Splash!

Take a bath

Here in the laundry tub.

Spin me around

Till I'm upside-down

And make our noses rub!

Splish! Splash!

Take a bath

Here in the kitchen sink.

Wash me up

With my sippy cup

Until I start to shrink!

Splish! Splash!

Take a bath

Here in the warm spring rain.

Hang me out

By the water spout

Until I'm dry again!

Splish! Splash!

Take a bath

Here in the big white tub.

Bubble me clean

Like a beauty queen

And wrap me in a hug!

Crib Critters

Out of the crib

    Teddy drops,

    Doggy plops,

    Lion falls,

    Monkey crawls,

    Dolly flips,

    Elephant slips,

    Kitty flies—

I stop and cry,

      wait,

      and when

Daddy picks them up

      and then

        leaves the room —

Quietly,

    silently,

      once again,

    Teddy drops . . .

Rocking

Rocking in this rocking chair,
I've grown so sleepy-eyed.
My momma's singing softly,
And Teddy's by my side.

I've got so much to see and do,
But I'm so warm and snug.
My momma's singing softly,
And Teddy needs a hug.

So I'll just close my eyes a bit—
The things to do will keep—
'Cause Momma's singing softly,
And Teddy's gone to sleep.